Tales of Feral Youth

Alan Harland

An imprint of Ricketts-White Design
Waterford

Tales of Feral Youth

an imprint of Ricketts-White Design, Waterford, CT U.S.A.
www.mecatepress.com www.rickettswhitedesign.com

Paperback ISBN 979-8-9882433-2-8
Hardback ISBN 979-8-9882433-3-5

Library of Congress Control Number: 2023918909

Cover Illustrations: Kimberly Miller Nadwairski
Cover and book design: Judy Ricketts-White

Published by Mecate Press, Ricketts-White Design, Waterford, CT.
Printed in the U.S.A.

To Helen.
You suggested that I should keep a journal (what a concept).
This is the result.

To Bob.
You gave freely something very valuable, your time.

To Kathleen and Jack,
for always being positive.

To my children.
I cannot put in words how much I love all of you.

Original Artwork

By

Kimberly Miller Nadwairski

To Judy.

With love and appreciation.

CONTENTS

INTRODUCTION

I started writing these stories after I was in a car accident and was unable to work in the manner that I had in the past. The next (scary) step was to actually have someone read what I had written. It became for me the most fun thing ever. To have someone read and enjoy (or offer critical evaluation about) my stories has become a defining part of my life. I never know when, or if, I will write. It's always a surprise when I write a story and I like it. I write because I love the people and things that I write about. They are a part of me. I have always written. On scrap paper, or in an old notebook that is now lost, the writings just disappeared. It wasn't until I reached out to someone that I knew had some background in literature, and asked her to evaluate some early stories. She made one suggestion; that I keep a journal of my writings. Honestly, the thought had never occurred to me. I would encourage anyone who writes to ardently save all that you write. Your story is important, even if no one else gets it.

TALES OF FERAL YOUTH

(a beginning)

I was very young. It was one of my first forays into the deeper woods alone. I had somehow eluded my mother's watchful eye (there were five others devising various means of escape also). I had been to this place with my brothers, and walked through a cut in a stone wall down a short path to a pond. As my view opened onto the water, I knew instinctively to freeze. I lowered myself slowly down to make myself less conspicuous, and watched. On a raft that neighborhood boys had built was a heron that had caught a large bullfrog, and was tearing it apart live to eat. My heart ached for the unfortunate frog, yet I held no malice toward the heron. I felt a revelation in my heart at having witnessed one small act in God's Great Nature.

QUAHOG

He slipped into the icy water and his feet felt the stones worn smooth in the sand. He then curled his toes and slid his feet sideways. Immediately he felt his prize. Ducking under the water he touched his toes and then dug. He put the live-stone into the bag he had tied to his waist while his feet were working again. Six more times and then out of the water. He ran the short trail to a sun-rock and sat, arms around his knees; the accumulated warmth of the jagged ledge, and the sun itself, penetrating his body until the shivering stopped. He selected a breaking-stone and expertly hit the shell, breaking only the top half. Peeling back the broken edges a sharp piece of the upper shell was used to scrape the contents into the bottom half, and then he slurped it into his mouth. As he chewed the soft stomach dissolved into his throat and the rest became a leathery wad that he worked on as he dressed and gathered his belongings. He would no longer have to depend on the meager winter stores in the village; He would now eat well all through the long good-season.

When he got back to the village he cooked the remaining live-stones and gave the stomachs to his grandmother, who could no longer chew well and had grown hungry during the past hard-season. The rest of his family all had a taste of the tougher meat and his sisters began the work of making wampum from the broken shells.

MATT

He was a shacker, come out of New Bedford. The captain of the boat that I was fishing had hired him on for the trip. He had had some trouble up there and was looking for a new start in a place where he wasn't known. In the day, if you could look a man in the eye and say you could cut fast and work hard you could always find a site.

When you were catching good and you took someone on like that you never knew what you would get, so he had to prove himself on a trip lasting for probably two weeks. For half share. If you were what you said you were then you got a permanent site and full share money.

New Bedford was known for cutters and he turned out to be the real deal. Knew how to work a boat and could cut like hell. That's what scalloping was. Haul back the gear every hour, pick the deck, and cut. Sometimes for days without sleep in whatever weather the ocean might give.

So we had this one guy on our crew who liked to ride you if he thought he could get away with it. Made him feel like a big shot I guess. So he started riding this guy Matt about everything he did, and Matt just took it. Never said a thing, just took it. And he was good crew. Anybody would want him for crew. But this guy kept riding him.

It was getting late in the trip, maybe day ten or eleven, and I had gone off deck into the galley to cook. Matt had been left on deck alone by this guy to cut the monkfish that were also caught in the dredges. And you never left a guy like that; you come off deck as a crew when the work was done. So as soon as Matt comes in to the room where we left our boots and oilers he's getting ridden by this guy again.

Now when you cut monkfish you have a twelve inch Dexter knife that is kept razor sharp to cut through a big bone just behind the head of the fish, and Matt still had his in his hand. And he turned, quick as a blink, and pinned this guy against the bulkhead with his forearm across his chest. Then he rested the knife on it just short of blood, and said very calmly, "I've been to prison; I'm not afraid to go back" and just as quickly released him.

I was in the ways to the galley and saw it; had never seen such terror in a man's face. And when it was over I said, "say, Matt, I got some grub ready; come in and get something to eat." And that was the end of it.

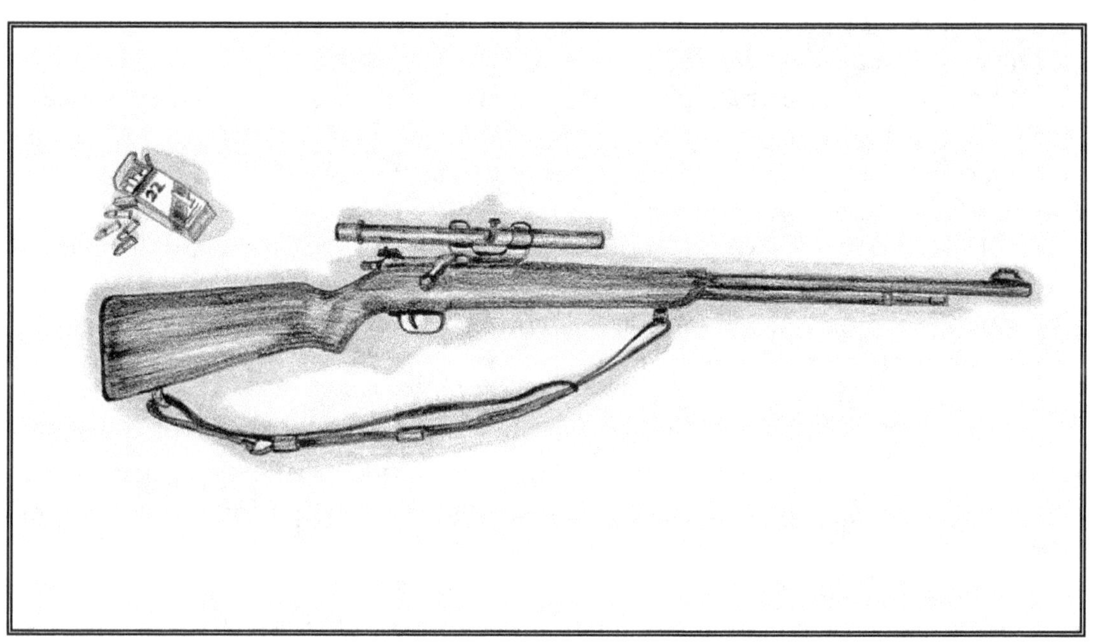

RIFLE

His father had left when he was young and now he was almost sixteen. They lived in a two room hovel with a shed built on one side. That was his room. The shack belonged to one of the "gentlemen" that his mother saw. She would come home after meeting with one of them with some meager supplies to keep things going; and now he saw his sister starting to run with some of the young men from town.

He sat now, in that room, admiring the greatest treasure he had ever known. The rifle was a .22 Remington and he had blued the barrel and rubbed the stock. It was a beautiful thing to behold. He had bought it, along with a cleaning kit and one hundred rounds, with a piece he had found on one of his forays into the foothills where he spent most of his time. A storekeeper who had known his father, and who knew the truth, traded fairly with him for the tiny pieces he had found before. Garnet also brought a little credit, but this was a real strike.

He would leave some food for his mother and take bags of raisins and grits on his next journey; but the rifle! All of his thoughts came back to it. It felt so natural when he held the stock to his cheek and looked down the sights. The sound of the bolt action was music, and he wouldn't waste any more rounds on practice, he knew he could shoot. The leather of the strap and the brass of the magazine slide were almost magical to him, and the pride that he felt in having made it his own was almost too much to absorb.

He had seen plenty of game during the shorter trips and the rifle, the raisins and the grits, and the pan that he also ate from were all that he needed to sustain and protect himself for longer trips into the wilder areas beyond the foothills. The garnet and the dust were dependable and now he knew of the treasure that could be found.

BIRD-WITH-MANY-SONGS

Quiet, thoughtful men, especially as they age, were respected in the village. There were plenty of rash, arrogant men to hunt and to protect the small community. The quiet-men preserved the teachings of the village and acted as ambassadors to other villages in the larger nation. Bird-With-Many-Songs was one such man. Much of his family had been killed by the disease that was brought by the men-who-always-wore-clothes. A son and two daughters had survived and he knew that they were the strongest and most able to resist the evil spirits that these strange men brought, and that even death was good in nature. His family was once again growing through these children and the pride that he felt gave honor to those who had perished.

His youngest daughter had survived but was changed by the fevers and never left her closest family. Her older sister doted on her and was now with child through a marriage with one of the more respected men-with-no-years in the village. Her name was Fawn-In-The-Mist and her husband was called Yellow-Feathers. The younger was known as Lovely-Beads because she would spend long hours alone making necklaces and pendants from the shell of the live-stone. Her sister had taught her to make these beautiful creations that added wealth and prestige to the family; and whenever she had to be left alone she worked tirelessly. Her work was admired by all who knew of it.

Names often changed with time and his son was known at present by the simple name of Quahog because he was always the first to brave the freezing water to harvest the live-stone when the hard-season was near its end.

Spiritual beliefs were simple and largely personal to the individual. The inner spirit of a person never dies but moves on at the appropriate time to be with those who have already passed. His mother, who had also survived, was known as Owls-Daughter and was happy to be near the time that she would reunite with those she had loved in the past.

CONSTANT

Quahog was watching a settlement that the men-who-always-wear-clothes were building. It was a particularly hot day and he wore only a leather loin cloth and a few of his most important tools; his bow, a crude knife made of a sharp stone, and of course his feathers, his spikes from his first kill, and his wampum; all of which gave him strength. He also had a small pouch that contained provisions for many days in the forest. He spent most of his time in the woods and on the waters but he would sometimes take time to watch these people to try to understand their ways. He knew that their fire-sticks were dangerous but it was easy to get close to the settlement undetected. His father was Bird-With-Many-Songs, a revered elder in the community and Quahog's reputation was growing because of his long absences and the knowledge he was gaining by his time spent alone in the natural world. The name his people had given to these settlers was derogatory; they could not understand why, as hot as it was, they always wore heavy outer garments.

His hearing was keen and he had come to understand some of their language and often practiced saying the words, trying to make sense of them. On this particular day he was observing a young boy he had often seen. He was weaker than most and was being beaten because he wasn't working hard enough in the small field that had been assigned to him. This made no sense to Quahog because his people nurtured the youngest and the weakest until they found the best way they could to serve the village. The boy was sweating heavily and was clearly being made sick by the heat and the work. Quahog pondered why he was not allowed to take off his clothing to get air to his body. When the beating was over and the man who administered it had left, the boy left the field and walked a short distance into the woods. This was a chance he had been waiting for. He knew the boys name was Constant and he approached unseen. Using a common greeting he had learned he revealed himself and said, "Constant; peace brother."

The boy was afraid but when Quahog went down on one knee and held out his hand, saying again, "peace brother," the boy was reassured and took his hand in the manner of his people. The bond was quickly made but the boy looked back at the field; torn between the known life of misery and the unknown. When Quahog said, "come: safe," the decision was made. They walked deeper into the woods, then approached a place where the forest opened up to the big-water. Quahog removed what little he carried and entered the water, coming out with several of the clams that were revered by his people and were the source of his name. Cracking open the shell and taking one into his mouth he offered one to Constant. The salty taste was unlike anything he had ever known and they ate several more. Then Quahog reentered the water and beckoned to Constant, saying "good." Constant took off his clothes and entered the cool water. The experience amazed him and he smiled for the first time. Exiting the water Constant put on only his light undergarments and shoes, leaving the rest at the water's edge. Quahog motioned that he should take them, making a shivering gesture to tell him they would be of use later when the hard-season came.

Quahog on his own could be back to his village in less than a day, but knew that it would take several at the slow pace necessary to not deplete Constant's strength. They took it easy for the rest of the day, making their way inland on a trail that led to the village. When evening came they camped next to a pond. Quahog built a small fire and caught several frogs; cutting off the legs and searing them on a rock next to the fire. The taste was amazing to Constant and they greedily ate all that was available. Quahog then took out a piece of the dried deer meat that was a staple of his people. Cutting it in half they slowly chewed it until it dissolved into their bodies. Quahog then made a crude bed out of leaves and pine needles and they lay next to each other and slept.

First light saw Quahog preparing for the day. He eliminated all signs of the fire and the camp he had made. Constant awoke and lay still for a while. He watched his new friend; the only one he had ever known. He arose and Quahog offered him another piece of meat and they rejoined the trail. They made good time until they reached a rocky rise that clearly put a strain on Constant. Quahog decided to stop and rest when they reached the top, knowing they could reach his village the next day. They set up camp and Quahog found a vantage point to hunt. Motioning with his hands for Constant to sit quietly, they waited. When a squirrel got close Quahog silently drew his bow. His arrow was true and they had another feast for the evening. They had also gathered some berries along the trail and these made a fine dessert. The next day's trail was easier and they made the outskirts of the village by late in the day. Quahog motioned for Constant to sit. He then said "good" and, pointing to himself, then to his village, then back to himself, and then to Constant, he told him to wait until his return. He then ran the short distance to the village. Finding his father, he told him of the events of the past few days. Trusting the instinct of his son they walked to where Constant waited. On the way Quahog told him of the greeting to give Constant, and they practiced it several times.

Bird-With-Many-Songs was a quiet but imposing man and when they reached the place where Constant waited he bent over, offered his large hand and said, "peace brother." For the first time in his life Constant knew the meaning of the words. When they entered the village it caused great interest among the people but the stature of Bird-With-Many-Songs made them to understand that this was a good thing, and Constant was welcomed by all.

ASSIMILATION

Quahog was slowly introducing Constant to the ways of the tribe and the forest but he had to range far in his quest for knowledge of the natural world, and often could not be held back by him.

Constant was gaining strength through Quahog's teachings but whenever he was not busy he would sit with Lovely-Beads; fascinated by the quiet simplicity of the work that she did. He would sit for hours with her and the bond between them was becoming strong.

The beautiful beads and pendants that they were now creating together were used by Bird-With-Many-Songs to honor and thank those who had contributed in some meaningful way to his family or to his village. The larger Nation of tribes and villages also knew of the work of Lovely-Beads and it was now in great demand, furthering the prestige of the family of Bird-With-Many-Songs.

LAUNDRY

It was an old fish-tote that my Grandfather used for his dirty clothes on his trips on the fishing boat. He would put his clothes and his sea-bag and assorted other items in it to bring them off the boat at the end of the trip. He would throw it up on the docks and with a long steel hook he would drag it from the boat to his truck to bring it home. My mother would lovingly empty it and wash the clothes in a washer we had just for his fish-clothes. She would then clean it and get things ready for his next trip. When it was empty, no matter how tired he was after weeks at sea, he would put me in the tote and hook it with the hook and drag me around and tell me that I was the captain of the best fishing boat in all of New Bedford. He would swing it wildly side to side and say that the seas were picking up and we were in for a real blow today. He would stop and bounce the tote up and down and say that we were hauling back the catch and that the work was just starting. And at the end he would slow down and say that this old tub would only make about eight knots even with a good tide. It smelled like fish and sweat and diesel fuel and the sea. It smelled like my grandfather.

WOLVES

He was chosen by his grandfather to accompany him when he went to be with the wolves. He was proud to have been selected but nervous about what he knew he would have to do. A small gathering was held the previous day, much like others he had known, and they were just now losing sight of the small village. The old man walked beside him when he could, but tired easily and rode on the small sled that the boy pulled for most of the way. The first thing he had said was, " do not be sad; you will soon see me again."

The sled held some provisions for the boy and a few of the old man's favorite possessions, but most of his belongings were left for those who remained in the village. It pulled easily even with the weight of the old man and they had made many miles when the light dimmed for a few hours, and they slept.

They proceeded quietly the next day. The old man was weakening but his determination was evident. His only words were, "the wolves will treat me well; I have left the remains of many kills for them to feast upon."

They had now reached their destination; a rocky expanse of hills from where the Elders continued their journey. The old man selected a place where the low sun shown on a rock behind him. His affection for the boy, and his desire to ease his burden, were evident as he took off his outer covering and placed it on the boy. Then, indicating the sled with his open hand he said, "these things are yours now, use them well. Go back to the village and tell them that my heart is glad." He then took off the charm that he had worn since he was a boy himself, and placed it around the boys neck; saying, "This came to me from my father; wear it always and it will protect you, as it has me, until I see you again. Go now, while I rest, and tell those in the village of this."

INSTINCT

He awoke without moving to a noise he had heard in his sleep. His eyes darted until he saw a movement. The deer had sensed his presence also. They remained frozen for some time and he accepted the fact that he could not gain an advantage to take the animal. He arose slowly and watched as the deer's eyes fixed on him; Then a leap and it was gone. From an instinctual understanding he thought to himself; what beautiful things exist in the forest, in a harsh balance that is divine in nature.

Three of Quahog's greatest possessions had come from his first kill. The meat was shared in the village but the hide and horns became his. The cover that he slept under, the small pouch that he tied to his waist, and the two charms made from the spike horns of the young animal were all made from it and gave him a new prestige that he felt growing inside of himself. He now wore around his neck the charms, the bead necklace that his sister had made from the shell of the livestone, and many feathers.

He reached into his pouch, which was also his pillow, and felt the three pieces of meat that were dried like leather. He put one piece into his mouth; the other two would allow him to stay another day in the forest, even if he found no other sustenance.

He now went to a running stream to freshen himself and to finish his morning meal with cool water. There was a growth of edible cress in the stream that he also ate, and he looked forward to the rest of the day, working some of the trees that had produced kills in the past. His bow had already proven itself and he would sit long hours in silent ambush, absorbing the forest into himself.

SHANGHAI (PETE)

He was good crew once you had him on the boat for a while, but right now you could hit him with a 2x4 and he wouldn't move. The captain had sent us to go find him because we were short crew, and we had found him at his brother's apartment out stone cold from the shit he had bought with his pay from the last trip. The human seagulls were always waiting for him when we came in from a trip because they knew he would have a nest in his pocket. Anyway, we wrapped him up in a blanket and dragged him across the floor and down the stairs and out to the truck. We threw him in the back and drove the short distance to the docks, backing up close enough to the boat to get the winch to it. Wrapping him up in some old netting sewn up with some twine like a purse, we hooked up the package to the winch line and swung it over onto the boat.

The operator of the winch wasn't exercising much patience at 4am and the bundle broke free, sailing across deck and bouncing off the stanchion for the net-reel. We all had a good laugh out of this as we dropped him in a pile on deck. We left him wrapped up in the net and the blanket and started to throw off the lines for the captain to begin the long steam out to the fishing grounds. We would lose a day or two out of him but by day three he would outwork most of us and be good crew for the rest of the trip.

SQUIRREL #1

The wind had been building for several hours and he had been frantically gathering a few seeds and nuts to sustain him through the storm. He was now high up the maple tree in the nest that he called home. It was an abandoned nest he had found that he had spent many hours rebuilding and he knew it was strong, but if it was a bad storm it would take all his effort to keep it from blowing apart. With the tree swaying violently he packed his stores in a pocket of leaves where the three main branches of his home came together. He ate a few maple seeds and then ran to the top of the tree where he rode one of the smaller branches, taking a look over his tree-top world. Then back to the nest to prepare for the night. Grabbing branches and pieces of nest with both front and rear paws, his grips locked; never letting go through his fitful sleep. In this manner he would try to preserve his home through the storm. It would be a long night.

SQUIRREL #2

The storm was coming on hard. I had gone into the galley to try to secure what I could in there, but now was back on deck with the rest of the crew, doing the best we could to work at lashing down everything that could move and stowing the catch in the fish-hold. It was getting real dangerous, with waves coming over the railing and washing across deck; and at times crashing over the wheel-house itself. Both the boat and crew were getting pretty beat up, and when we finally got off deck we found our places in the wheel-house to try to hold on. The captain and the mate got the two chairs that commanded the boat. Either the engineer that serviced the engines that kept the boat working, or the cook who supplied the boat and tried to feed the crew would get the chair at the chart-table. The deck-boss liked the small bench built into the side of the table. The rest of the crew found corners and things to hold onto in an attempt to not get thrown when the boat took one of the enormous crests badly. Creative uses of rope were employed to tie off bodies, and survival suits were piled where they could be accessed quickly. The captain and mate did their best to keep the bow into the wind and waves so that the boat didn't get rolled by a hard side-sea. There would be no sleep. It would be a long night.

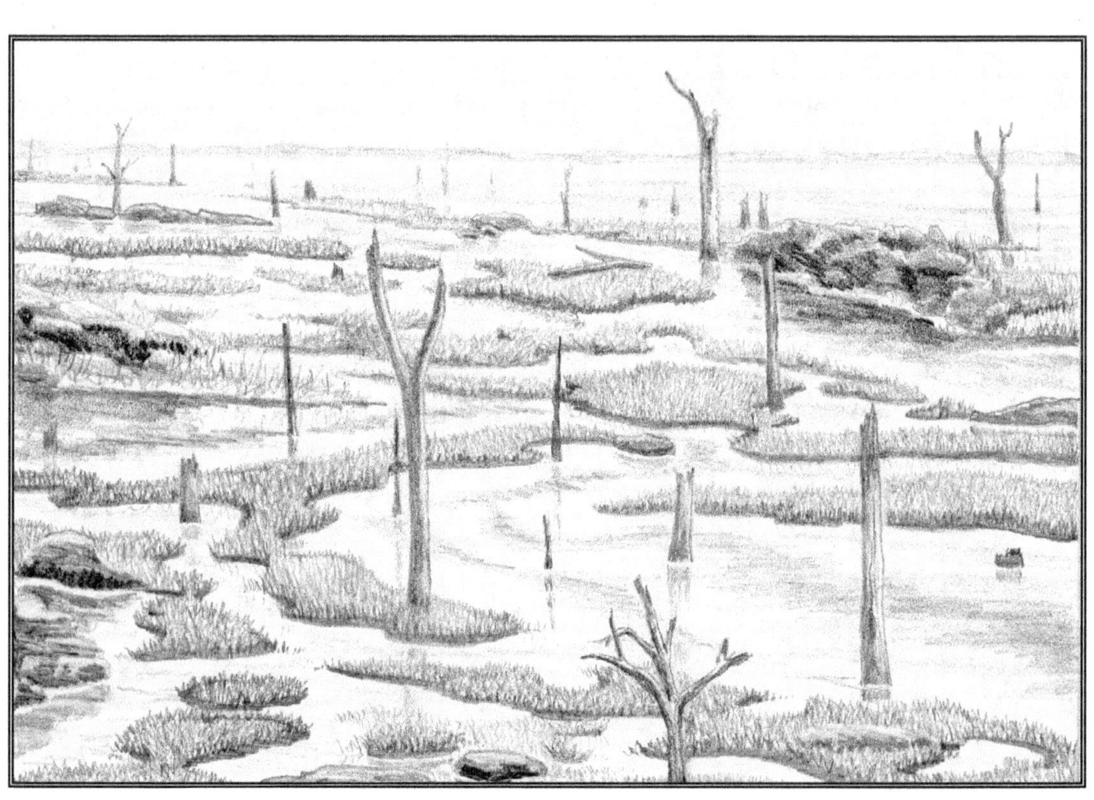

HIGHWAY

In places Quahog made marks on the trail that only he could see. He used the sharp- club he had made from a piece of fractured granite and a short length of strong oak branch. An elder had shown him how to affix the head to the shaft with a strip of skin that was his reward when he had found a deer carcass. The meat was bad but the hide and antlers were harvested and a piece of the hide had become his as tribute for his contribution to the village. The club had become a great possession; an invaluable tool that never left his side. He was now making his way far into a region known in the language of his village as swamp-that-can-not-be-crossed.

He was three days away from the village. The first day he had eaten the live-stones he had brought; cracking the shells and savoring the cool, salty taste. From the second day on there was an array of small edibles available as he reached the edges of the wetland. Frogs and snakes and a few berries and grains would now sustain him.

Making his way into the clearings where the mire was deepest, and held only dying frames of trees, he was able to make his way along islands created by the drought of an unusually dry good-season. Here he crossed and re-crossed many times to make sure he knew the way; the skeletal trees and the ever present granite outcroppings, now fixed in his memory, were his guide.

He worked deeper and deeper in; several times reaching an impasse where he would have to turn back to start a new route; getting steadily closer to the dry ground that he knew existed in the direction of where the sun sets during the longest days of the good-season.

Not of any clear thought process, but of an inborn instinct he knew he was getting closer to his destination. He saw the dry woods appearing far ahead and his pace began to quicken.

Finally back among the big trees he felt more at home, and soon he had found a small connector to the main trail that went many miles around the swamp to other small villages of the larger nation. He knew this place as part of the network that connected the entire region. His heart raced as he turned and ran back over the trail. This new highway would save several days on the journey around the swamp on the trail that left his village in the direction of moss-on-trees.

He ran and leaped and slopped his way over the now familiar ground, excited by the thought of the tribute he would receive when he showed the elders of the village this new trail. He would soon be working with other men-with-no-years from the region to build up the trail with logs and stones, becoming an invaluable route for trade and social gatherings among the villages.

LUCKY

I had an old fisherman one time tell me that having a seagull shit on you was good luck. Now he was as smart as I've seen regarding things on the water but I must say I was sceptical about this particular piece of nautical knowledge. When I asked how this could be he would never tell me why, said I'd figure it out myself someday. It was one day when I was on deck by myself and we weren't catching very well and not making very much money and things were a little rough at home and I was filling stinking bait barrels full of skates to sell to the lobstermen for their traps when I got hit again. I guess it don't get much lower than I was feeling at that moment when it occurred to me. It don't get much worse luck as when you get shit on by a seagull and my luck must surely be getting better.

LEAP

They had seen so many others before. Her symptoms were just starting to appear but they knew what the outcome would be. The disease that the men-who-always-wore-clothes had brought had decimated the small community, affecting some while others seemed immune.

He was a son of Bird-with-many-songs and his name was Winding-stream. Her name was Harvest-moon and she lived in a nearby village. The villages approved of their meetings and on this day they made love in increasingly intimate ways at a place in the forest that had become theirs. They then parted, tomorrow's meeting thoughtfully planned.

The next day they met and again made love. When their bodies were satisfied they made their way to the trail that led to the top of a hill where a steep drop was formed by an immense piece of granite that had separated from the main cliff eons ago. They held each other and cried for the last time and then looked into each other's eyes. Then turning and running together across the crest of the hill they reached the edge.

When land gave way their spirits soared while their soon to be lifeless bodies clawed at each other to achieve one final embrace, flying out into an eternity of time and space.

Save for
Michael
2LB.

CAN

I had saved the can earlier in the week and it was a good one. Big coffee cans were always the best and with a cover you could put stuff in it too. I was now in an old Thompson lapstrake boat with a Mercury outboard, that to this day remains the most beautiful boat that I have ever seen. The varnished ribs and the white caulking between the wooden strips on the bow were kept in immaculate condition, and as my father laid the boat over on one of the large bends in the river my hand felt the power of the splash along the side of the boat.

After he had set the bow line in deep water, I eagerly jumped over the side to run a line to the beach. Last year he had to throw me over because I was scared, but now I was proud to be able to help. As soon as we hit the beach I was free, and a world of adventure awaited. We were on a spit of land with one side aweather and one side alee. We anchored on the protected side and there was frequently a large surf on the other. At the far end of the spit was an old concrete military installation half buried in the sand, built for wars of long ago. There were groups of people along the beach and when a boy my own age asked about the can, and I told him what it was for, I had made a friend.

We made our way down the beach to a grouping of rocks to tear off clusters of mussels. The tide was still too high to dig for clams, but he caught a good sized blue crab and we put that in the can along with the mussels.

Then back to where our families had set up. A large coal pit had been built with driftwood to cook on. We emptied the can on the beach and set some salt water to boil on the coals. Pliers and foil that I had brought in the can were cover and handle. As we waited we practiced catching the crab as it tried to escape. Running sideways and clicking its claws together it was a formidable foe.

With the water now boiling, in went first some mussels, then the crab, then more mussels. When the steam sputtered under the foil we knew it was done. With the can held by the pliers and cooled quickly in the cold sea water, our meal was ready. Tearing off the top shell of the crab and cracking the body in two, we each got half. The mussels were shared with some boys who had been watching us, and the shell of the crab was kept by my friend as a treasure.

RACE

The race was called in the usual way. One of the oldest and boldest of the men-with-no-years had announced that he would run to the top of a hill that carried a sacred mysticism in the history of the village. All of the bravest youth of the village were now hopping up and down and making sounds, and painting their faces and bodies with dyes that their families produced from the wealth of the forest. Races could be called at any time and the caller had run third in the race that was held in the thaw of the previous hard-season. Great tribute would come to him if he won. The village would not condemn him if he lost, but the embarrassment would steel him to greater challenges to come. The pack now started moving toward a trail that led to the first rises and then to a steep ascent to the top of the hill. As the pace quickened they spread out and started to plan their individual strategies and routes for the race. There were many paths to take to attain the summit and they all knew this area well.

Quahog was at a pace with the leading runners and was just now starting to feel the pounding in his chest that would give his body the strength to propel him to the top of the hill. He saw other runners through the trees on either side of him, but none with a decided advantage, and as the leaders were nearing the final ascent he sensed without looking back the presence of someone directly in back of him.

Now into the steepest sections and using roots and rocks and branches and trees as a means to transport himself up the incline, he was prepared. When he felt the hand grab his ankle (which was an acceptable maneuver, using a leg the same as any other natural hold to gain an advantage) he instinctively turned while grabbing a branch, and kicked with his other leg. It was not a hard blow but it met its mark, rubbing dirt into the eye of his assailant. The grip was released and he was quickly back in the race.

Pressing ever harder as he neared the goal he saw two runners from different trails gain the peak simultaneously and then one more just ahead of him as he also reached the final pinnacle, leaping high into the air and letting out a cry of victory, as the others had before him, and as all others behind him would also do.

SILENCE

Silence was his greatest weapon. If he could also position himself downwind of the great animal he would eliminate its two strongest powers. Hearing and smell were good in the deer, but its eyesight was poor so Quahog was positioned well; with a little cover from a dead tree trunk and a thicket of brush. He knew from watching in the past that many deer passed this way on a run that narrowed between two ridges of solid granite and led to a stream that did not dry in the good-season when the land became hard.

His silence, and his patience and perseverance often were not enough, but today all of the blessings of the natural world seemed to be with him. It was the time when the antlers were large and had just shed the velvet of this year's growth. It was also the time of year when the females were in estrus and the males were incautious to everything but finding a mate; fighting to be the one to continue a superior bloodline overcame usual instincts.

As the deer edged closer the boy heard two things happening. The first was the clacking of the horns of another animal on a sapling a ways off from where he was. The second was the first animal stomping its forefeet and letting out a loud snort. Thoughts of taking the animal were gone because he was still too far for an accurate shot and instead he wondered how this drama would play out.

As the deer moved closer to each other they held their antlers high and displayed their size and strength, pawing the earth in a prancing action that was majestic to see. When they were within a few feet of each other they snorted and stomped one last time, then lunged as if on cue. Antlers locked and twisted as clods of dirt flew from their hooves from the power of the collision, and a wheezing, grunting noise was made as they tried not to expend their air too quickly. An advantage was gained by one, and the other was thrown to the ground, with the impetus sending the first past the now-unprotected animal. It turned and attacked the exposed belly with antlers lowered in an attempt to rip at the vulnerable underside. The deer on the ground was just able to hook the antlers with one of its hind legs and turn, gaining traction with its forelegs. It was lifted awkwardly into the air but maintained its footing enough to rapidly retreat from the battle. The first started to give chase and then stopped; he had won and was satisfied with his victory.

SUNDOWN

I never usually counted the catch to try to figure out how much money I was making, but I couldn't help myself. We were on a jag, right when we needed it the most. We couldn't even get out to fish most days in mid January, but the weather forecast looked good for days ahead and me and John on the Seafarer and Pete and Joey on the Miss Karyn had made a rush decision to steam far enough to the south'rd to try to find the fluke. We had left at ten the night before to drop our gear at first light.

The day saw some of the biggest hauls I had seen on the Seafarer and I knew Pete's crew Joey was counting too. Big fluke were everywhere and I knew prices were high because the smaller boats couldn't usually get out to fish in the harsh winter conditions. We were also loading up on whiting and squid and some really nice scup. I hadn't had a decent pay in weeks and this was just what we all needed to get us through the winter until fish started showing up closer to home.

Days were short this time of year and we were just taking back the nets on the sundown tow. It wasn't even really that cold either, with no spray due to the lack of any real wind. As soon as we got this load on deck John would turn the boat and head for home. I would work the deck alone this tow but I didn't even mind; I was on top of the world and being tired didn't even occur to me. This was what fishing was all about: all the work to keep the boat fishing, all the trips just trying to scratch out a pay, all the sacrifice your family made because you chose to be a fisherman, all came together on this one glorious day of fishing. I had my hand on the lever that ran the net drum, winding up the net just like I had a thousand times before and I stole a look at the sun just creeping below the horizon and the sky so beautiful that my words could never fully describe. Days like this were rare and a sense of perfection had crept into my soul, and I knew that John was sitting with his feet up on the wheel talking to Pete on the radio, trying hard not to let his excitement show.

So there I was with the bag of fish at the end of the net just breaking the surface and the hydraulics pressurizing with the weight when I heard what sounded like a rifle shot. The lever went dead and the net drum reversed. John quickly had the boat in neutral and I knew what I had to do next. There is a slot cut in the side of the drum with a heavy chain and hook on the stanchion that I had to slam into the slot to stop the net from running out. I accomplished this with my hand still attached and quickly looked on deck for where the breach in the hydraulic lines might be. John was already out of the wheelhouse and into the engine room to check the lines there. When he came out and our eyes met we both knew. The only other lines went through the fish hold to the stern of the boat. He tore open the cover to the hold below deck and we heard the hissing of the last of the pressure exiting the lines. The catch was ruined. The life drained out of us like the fluid drained out of the lines. From that point on we were numb to anything but the heavy sense of disappointment while performing the work necessary to get the boat heading for home. Towing the heavy bag of fish behind the boat we could only make about three knots and it seemed like it took forever to get back to the docks. I don't think two words were said between us during the whole trip home. As we were nearing the harbor we saw the Miss Karyn heading back out. They had already taken out their catch and were heading back out to load up again. John and I spent the next two days cleaning up the mess and repairing the hydraulic lines and by the time we were done the weather had closed back in and we never got another chance.

LUCY

While not of the Feral Youth genre I wanted to include this story.

I met Lucy when we had to place my mom in a nursing home. I was blessed to have been able to alter my schedule to spend a lot of time there with her. In two years visiting I never saw anyone come to visit Lucy and I tried to be pleasant to her, but she was a handful. She was a terror to the girls that worked there, she swore like a sailor, and if she got close enough to you in her wheelchair she would sometimes try to slug you for no apparent reason. When I would try to leave through the locked doors she would follow me and try to escape, screaming "let me out, let me out." She would call me names that I had seldom heard when I worked on fishing boats and with one hand try to grab the door and with the other try to belt me a good one. It was so bad that I had to ask the girls who worked there to protect me, which of course they made fun of me about. She had a little stuffed monkey that she kept with her all the time in her wheelchair and in her bed. I must say I began to look forward to her antics as an enjoyable distraction during my visits to my mom.

It was getting near the end for my mom and family was gathering. I was in the doorway to her room talking to a sister who had just arrived when Lucy appeared. I did not know what to expect and knew that my sister was totally unprepared for the assault that may occur when she held out her stuffed monkey, the only thing that she loved in the world, and said, "give this to her, I don't need it," and when I hesitantly took it she quickly spun her wheelchair around and left. It is not within my power to express the emotion that I felt at that time, and I can't think of a more generous act of kindness or a more profound gift than Lucy's little monkey.

CORN

(not an ending)

I was working in my back land that overlooks the hay field that opens up to where the cow corn is grown. A rustling in the corn had caught my attention. My first thought was that a large animal was passing through the field, but it soon became apparent that it was a group of boys that were doing the damage. As I was debating whether to call the land-owner, or to run out there myself, the destruction stopped. I was angry that these disrespectful children would ruin the product of a mans hard work like they did, and was just starting to walk across the field to survey the damage when I heard a loud "whoop" and then many more cries of battle as two seperate groups of boys came together in mortal combat. The ears of rock-hard cow corn became grenades; the stalks, with a ball of dirt still attached by the roots, became deadly maces that exploded when they struck; the stalks then became whips that they gleefully struck each other with; and at the end of the fray they all fell to the ground, exhausted and laughing and just starting to assess their wounds. How I longed to be one of those boys. To have felt the joy of youth instead of the anger of an old man. And I set back to my work having learned a lesson; I hope a better man for it.

www.ingramcontent.com/pod-product-compliance
Lightning Source LLC
Chambersburg PA
CBHW081139300726
48982CB00006B/1005

* 9 7 9 8 9 8 8 2 4 3 3 3 5 *